TRISAGION OF DEATH

Mireya Robles

Translated by Susan Griffin in

collaboration with the author

Order this book online at www.trafford.com
or email orders@trafford.com

Most Trafford titles are also available at major online book retailers.

Note for Librarians: A cataloguing record for this book is available from Library and Archives Canada at www.collectionscanada.ca/amicus/index-e.html

Printed in Victoria, BC, Canada.

ISBN: 978-1-4269-2420-0 (Soft)

Trafford rev. 1/15/2010

 www.trafford.com

North America & international
toll-free: 1 888 232 4444 (USA & Canada)
phone: 250 383 6864 ♦ fax: 812 355 4082 ♦ email: info@trafford.com

CONTENTS

TRISAGION OF DEATH

Today she said that she would never reconcile herself with life.

The Grand Cardinal passed by, spilling incense. Her hands shed their flesh until the bones were clean, ready to be interred. Absurdly, she held a posy of violets in one of her broken hands: "I wanted to be born for you this particular Spring, before another went by. In this particular Spring in which I endured the Bath of the Possessed and I purged myself and cleansed myself and something undecided in the atmosphere told me that I had been born again. I am one of these violets, I am three, I am all of them, I am flowers. Spring, violets, two, three, posy, I was born". She went spitting nonsense into the air and all the psychiatrists' couches became ineffectual.

The fumes from the incense began their diabolic dance. The Grand Cardinal chanted: "Holy, holy, holy" and carefully marked the rows in which the dead would be laid.

This Dwarf of Destiny paraded her tragic flowers. Everyone had seen her destiny and could point to it with their index fingers. No-one forgave her for the botched abortion and when she was born whole, defending herself without knowing it for nine months, everyone continued to view her as something still to be completed, an embryonic foetus which still lacked the odd stitch, three fasteners, five or six cuts, a piece of skin. No-one could discern your leprosy in the very centre of your navel. All the prehistoric animals swallowed the attempt to exterminate you with an insecticide. The forceps refused to take the air from your lungs and floating, blind, in the womb, you began to poison all those who could have been your brothers and sisters.

"Holy, holy, holy" shouted the Cardinal's silks and the precious stones on his hands filled with earth: "In this corner, touched by my hands, three corpses will fit. Three of the most illustrious dead, the first three fatalities in the Great War".

The Dwarf's fattest and most deformed finger touched the mound of earth and rage rose in the holy silks. The Dwarf, who had materialised on her own to be forever alone amongst the others, was not aware of the Great Rejection. She stopped. Ethereal and solemn, with arms outstretched, she began to vomit up the sermon that she believed was destined for all her brothers and sisters. A wave of semiconsciousness told her that no-one had been able to make out her leprosy in the centre of her navel. It was the hour of the holy-holy-holy ground and all would know how to locate her sores in this vomit of truth. Ethereal and solemn, with her arms outstretched, she began to launch her nonsense into the air: "And afterwards I went out into the earth and only through the word of others did I absorb through my nails the mark of my prehistory. The menacing foetus lost the word and I perceived fear in the voice of the centaur. In some corner of my forehead the mark is to be found. Fingers come apart without touching it and all look at it without seeing it. The passage of Time stumbles in my throat and no-one saw me in the act of devouring myself, daughter of myself. It is important that you recognise my echo in every back: you will find it, dead, in any trace of sand. All the horizons swallow the waves of my voice. I am the non-realization and I return, minute, to my seed. Do not allow the starving doves to devour the corn of my hands. They have swallowed the stones of my blood and I was left uselessly dispersed through the air". Ethereal, ecstatic, mystical, the Dwarf grew for an instant to the height of her peers. The excavations continued at a frenetic rhythm and no-one could measure her size. The terrible hour of classification had arrived. The Grand Cardinal mentioned the Great War: "We all have to go, we all should go, it is our obligation, but anyone who, through an act of individual will, has gone to the Great War, will be left without a resting place in the holy-holy-holy ground". The Dwarf of Destiny listened to all of this without understanding and thought that, in this enthusiasm to collect and classify the dead she should offer herself up as the first fatality. And she grew invisible to everyone else, making the voices that would come from the others, echo in her ears: "We already have, we already have our first fatality". She did not know what suicide was. She did not know that to decide not to live is to commit suicide. She did not know that no-one granted her the right to death and that in death-suicide she would be as isolated as she had been from that placenta where she had only heard the voices and groans that formed her prehistory.

When her hands had shed their flesh and her bones were ready to be interred, she did not recognize Death's Great Rejection. And she felt the premonition of Spring on the nerve endings of her skin. The blessed ones deserving of the holiness of that "Holy, holy, holy" ground had remained behind. And they stole from her the dignity to choose her death. And she did not realise that her sermon was swallowed by the wind and that the stones of her blood continued uselessly dispersed throughout the air. And believing herself invested with the solemnness of death, she dragged her sandals in a way that imparted a certain rhythm of beauty to her threadbare ankle-length skirts. In the dense heat of midday she flooded those streets with her song: "I wanted to be born for you this particular Spring, before another went by. This particular Spring in which I endured the Bath of the Possessed and I purged myself and cleansed myself and something undecided in the atmosphere told me that I had been born again. I am one of these violets, I am three, I am all of them, I am flowers. Spring, violets, two, three, posy, I was born".

And she believed that she launched the definition of herself in these words. Wandering, she carried on without knowing that the whirlwind swallowed her voice, always filled with pain. She believed herself to be the bearer of her own message. And for this reason she did not understand the smiles on the faces of the children nor the light of the night owls in their eyes.

BALLAD IN PROSE

It is time to hide oneself. I have been, I am Roberto, I am the buyer-seller of the powder compact. I am the unicorn, I am the reader and I narrate. It is time to put things right. It is time for corrections. And I will be... your wife. I regress myself to sixteen years of age. I will marry you and I will bear your children. I wait for you each afternoon. I snap myself with your verses in the languor of my breasts that await your caresses. In the movement of the swing I drank your tears and I kissed your broken arm. A hug stops my breath and marks me with bells that sound like goodbye. My fingers, caught up with yours, begin breaking the contact. You move away in the night and you shout a goodbye to me that doesn't leave your lips. "Wait, wait, sailor of destiny. I will give birth to your sons. One, dark, with thick, black hair, with a smooth, rosy little mouth. He will be playful. Wait, wait, sailor of the night. I will bear your children..."

Devastating Time wants to erase the image of your white shirt beaten against the dark wind of midnight. Rested, with deep grooves around the mouth, wearing a housecoat, in a studio where one breathes in the sweet aroma of a deaf success still to come or which has already been or which occurred and then was over. "Outside, outside..." Rodrigo is no more and I am not Urraca. But

Trotaconventos is indeed here. Bent over herself, her hands misshapen by arthritis, allowing to escape from among her many threadbare and dirty skirts an acrid smell of urine. Diamond thief, wealthy smuggler, with four sons borne to you by a jewess like you. The hard tongue of the go-between, like that of a dying parakeet, moves desperately, sketching words: "He is Rodrigo, he is Calisto, you are Urraca, old loves, old friendship, a telephone call. Calisto is dying. You are Melibea, pray for his teeth, he is dying for you". The dun coloured wind of the night immobilises me in the doorway. He is Rodrigo, he is Calisto. Perhaps his white shirt is there, floating against the black of the night. But the fresh air is not fresh, the shirt is not a shirt, Rodrigo is not Rodrigo and Calisto is not Calisto. And Melibea... has a womb full of sand. And the son I was going to bear you never got skin nor touched your hands, nor urinated in a diaper. "Rodrigo... Rodrigo... I don't know, good woman, who Rodrigo could be... Calisto, Calisto... I don't know, good woman, who Calisto could be". She took herself off wrapped up in her covers, she took herself off wrapped in skirts and old urine. The door cried as it closed and, in my right hand, I grew a flower.

IN THE LAND OF SMOKE

Large room. Smoke. Open smiles. An atmosphere of music about to start. Skirts, orchids, evening gloves, diamonds, cigarette holders. The perfume of clean uniforms. Music about to burst forth. There she is, playing her part. Did she come with me? Will she leave with me? I don't know. There she is, apparently fitting into the mechanism of evasion. A glass of beer, cider, champagne. Smoke. Conversations, voices. Conversations in voices that don't seem to belong to the speakers. That emerge echoing like an empty box. As if those speaking were trying to escape from themselves in the resonance of their vocal cords. Smoke, voices, elegance becomes fabric. The glare of diamonds, the breadth of the smiles. A mass that slowly becomes ethereal, amorphous, and begins to blend with the smoke. A mass that elegantly, kindly, playfully seems to crowd around me. My chest becomes tight, the viscera of my heart thicken. I ought to slide out. Out of that mass that, loaded with indifference and with a lack of intention, seems to strangle me.

I find myself in a room I recognise. In a room where one watches television without listening to it, where one reads a book without absorbing its content. A sleeper couch, a television set, a wall of glass, two comfortable chairs. A clean room. An artificial ambience. An ambience of plastic leaves, garlands and flowers. Without thinking, I approach the artificial vegetation and try to inhale the absent perfume. Through an association of ideas a scene, buried in Time, in a land of snow and snowfalls and subzero temperatures, comes to mind. The steam from a cup of coffee caresses my lips. A coffee shop, a bar counter, a bar decorated in the Spanish style. To the right of my table, a low wooden wall full of flower pots with artificial flowers, leaves and garlands. My companion went up to the plastic vegetation and tried to absorb the absent perfume. Giving me an explanation that I did not ask for, she said: "How industriously the human being tries to dream. In this arid land, of ice, he preserves the greenery of a plant that does not exist". I felt an immense compassion towards human beings. Towards human beings who cover their destiny in a perfumeless green. The memory of this scene vanished from my mind but it left me with a strange taste on my lips, an odd sensation in my chest.

To the right of this artificial room, a doorway. A door that leads to the master bedroom. A small group of three women crowd into the entrance. One is of advanced years, another is a young woman who, without knowing how, I recognise as, or sense is the hostess. The third is a woman whose outline escapes the plane of reality for me. A third woman whom I cannot define. The old voice requests permission to go to the bathroom and losses itself in the doorway to the master bedroom. I remain seated on the couch, waiting for the group to go past me, indifferent, and leave me in the peaceful anxiety of this complete absence from everything, except myself. I wait for the moment when I will be left alone with the flowing of my blood, with the beating of my heart, with my thinking world. The hostess picks up a book. Standing, next to me, she begins to read. From time to time she looks at me and I incline my head as if meaning to say to her: "I have assimilated everything". Why is she reading to me? Does she consider it her duty to entertain me? My whole consciousness is concentrated on the atmosphere in the master bedroom. What an irresistible attraction! How do I explain it to the others? How do I explain this unstoppable attraction for that room to myself? Impatient because the old woman still has not come out, I try a joke: "Has that woman gone down the toilet?" The laughter I expected never rang out. The two women before me did not appear to be aware of my attempt at humour. The one who was reading interrupted me brusquely and showed me a word: HORDE. Pronouncing it out loud, she asked me: "Do you know what it means?" I answered her: "I don't know what it means when it is pronounced in that manner. I don't know what it means when it is written with that H that I hardly recognise". "It means -I wrote down- the relation of one word with another". While I accepted and made note of that nonsense, I felt ashamed of myself.

The old voice went past us and, showing a complete disinterest in the reading, she moved away, disappearing into the room of evasion. I told myself that a burning sensation was running around my bladder. Firmly and resignedly interrupting the reading, I said: "I need to go to the bathroom". The hostess shut the book. She drew a smile on her face. Without looking at the silhouette of the other woman, the indistinct person who was always at her side, I left the couch and I walked slowly towards the bedroom. A soft carpet of Prussian blue. Mediterranean furniture, dark wood. A taffeta bedspread. Blue and lilac stripes. A full-size bed, a double bed. Such intimacy! Such mystery! Standing, inspecting everything with my eyes. Wanting to pull the sound of hoarse voices from the silence. Wanting to draw the burning taste of kisses from the void. Delve, delve, look for the mark of the cry that escapes from between tense hands. The wardrobe... clothes take us close to experiences. I walked towards it. On the floor, some long nylon stockings, a girdle and a silken slip. Without touching the half-open door of the wardrobe, I stick my head in to look at the clothes. Skirts, blouses, coats, dresses.

The noise of machine guns firing pulled me from this introspection. I left the bedroom. The hostess, without asking my opinion, took a strong grip on my arm and began to run with me, leaving the house. The indistinct woman followed us. I tried to think and was not able to coordinate my ideas. It occurred to me that <u>she</u> remained behind. There, in the room of evasion. My intention was trapped in the strong iron of reality. Uniforms, machine guns, a jeep. War. Chinese, Chinese, Chinese. Uniforms. Bullets, shooting, machine guns. A white façade. A house built of masonry. The hostess calls for help. A Chinese woman appears and points to us with her finger. She denounces us. The hostess, addressing herself to the official at the jeep, tries to imitate the nasal monosyllables. A shield of feigned acceptance or integration that can save our lives. The machine gun aims. The hostess sets off at a run followed by the indistinct woman. I am petrified for a moment. I try to follow them. Noise. My chest is open, I bleed. <u>She</u> has remained in the room of evasion and I... I ought to go on and lose myself in the mist.

THE TRAY OF HOT CHOCOLATE

A run-down café used by Time. Used by thousands of beer drinkers who clinked their mugs of thick crystal with a merry spark in their eyes and who, without saying anything, wanted to say: "Cheers! I drink to you, because you're here, alive and happy". Small tables, very small, square, with red and white checkered clothes. All the tables, cramped so closely together so that one can hardly pass between them. The café is small and square like a room in a house. The walls are all of glass and through them one sees a village that is not a village but a beach; or a beach that is not a recreational beach, but a fishermen's village. The sun, the light of the sun, is thick, yellow, and dense and enters the café from the beach ignoring the small concentrations of mist and leaving alone the constant humidity. As if heating or drying were not important, only showering the café with its torrent of heavy and brilliant light.

I enter on my own, without knowing why, without knowing where I come from nor how I arrived there. Only that moment is important. A moment in which I penetrate the world where one talks and laughs. I don't hear what they are saying. They are unintelligible murmurs followed by laughter that seems sincere because it comes from deep inside, as if pushed by the diaphragm, laughter located a little above the stomach. This is not laughter which is artificially produced with forced, guttural sounds. There is nowhere to sit down. There is no place for me in this cramped, dirty, brilliant world of those who laugh. Without finding a seat, almost without looking for one, I see myself, suddenly, in the middle of my paused surprise, seated, waiting. I say, (because it has to be this way, because it cannot be otherwise), that I am twenty years old. Maybe I was sixteen, maybe seventeen or eighteen. An ancient, mature burden of solitude that I carry with me despite myself, tells me that I must be twenty years old.

I don't know who I'm waiting for, nor for what I'm waiting. I know that from these aged, sweaty sailors with large cracks in their faces, with their gratuitously feverish eyes, with their dirty, blue turtle-necked sweaters, with their knitted caps, with their spontaneous laughter that responds to nothing, from them I can expect nothing. I look for nothing in them. Perhaps it is only the desire to listen to laughter that holds me even if that laughter is only a gratuitous sound.

Ronald walks past my table several times. He is tall, strong --if he were a truck driver I would say he was well built--, his body is thick and wide, his hair is ash brown, slightly curly, burnt by the sun, in his eyes is a fleeting spark that seems to announce a smile which never quite arrives on his lips. It's him, he's the one I'm waiting for. He studies Medicine somewhere else. He's not the owner of the café nor is he a servant and yet, he has for that place, for these people, for that moment, an inexplicable importance. I should say, I must say, something forces me to believe that, if it were not for Ronald, that moment would not exist. And with the missing moment, the café, the beer and the laughter would disappear.

Ronald walks past me and I feel his presence, but he does not approach me. Ronald ought to know that it is him that I am waiting for. How is it possible that, with me on my own, seated, the only woman amongst so many aged men who smell of shellfish, he could not know that I am waiting for him? How is it possible that I am aware that there is no-one else to choose, that I must wait for him and that he is ignoring his own situation which is the same as mine? Or perhaps it is not the same situation. When I leave this run-down café I return to my defeated parents, to the dirt, to the daily hopes that die without being born, drowned in the absence of possibilities.

There I am, set into that seat, for an unmeasurable period of time, of days or minutes, or perhaps of a whole life accumulated in one instant of waiting. It seems an eternity from the last time that Ronald walked by my table. I must find out, I must know. Near me, there is a stout woman, around fifty years old, still with a young face, dressed all in black, with big blue or greenish shiny eyes. She is sobbing. She sobs inconsolably, she sobs with the despair of someone who knows that no-one can console her. I speak to her, feeling myself near her, but without moving any nearer. I know, without her having to tell me, that it has something to do with Ronald. I know, without her having to tell me, that it's about that strapping youth that walked by me, the one that never reached my table and the one to whom I had so often imagined myself telling my name and hearing him tell me his. "It's Ronald" -- she said to me. And I knew then that Ronald was him and that he had been lost. A war, I thought, I often imagined him dying in a war. "One more of life's absurdities" --she continued. "A bullet that someone fired for no reason. He felt himself with his right hand, the pain in his left shoulder, then he searched for it in his chest, his hand filled with blood and he fell down dead". I knew that she had to have another son and I asked after him.

"That one is fine, he'll be here soon". I stayed there, waiting for the other son without asking his name. I knew Ronald's name after his death. This one's name was unnecessary. The woman dressed in black disappeared from my surroundings. Because she was a vision or because she couldn't cry in that café of laughter or because she ceased to be important at that moment in my life.

Soon, very soon, the other one began to walk by. Seventeen, eighteen, perhaps. Thick and strong, but it would never have occurred to me to call him well built. Straighter hair, black, big, chestnut eyes, dark skin with a silky gleam. This one seemed to understand, this one understood at once and soon we found ourselves in an emptier room where the presence of others was hardly important. He reclined on the sofa, me at his side, I put my arms around his waist and rested my head on his chest. That was all. Life, after all, might not be a constant, difficult alienation. Perhaps it is possible to live like that, resting on a chest that one has to search for, that one has to find and wait for death. Perhaps life is not so difficult, perhaps it is not a constant, painful, separation.

I had my eyes closed so as to relax and rest in my destiny, but something inexplicable made me open my eyes slowly. I saw you there, in an easy chair, before me, looking at me with a resigned surprise and with a sadness that had only been, up till then, mine. You were calm and without words, I would have said that you reserved for me, a gesture of compassion. On your face was an exhaustion that looked just as if you had stolen it from me. You were close, with all the immenseness of your mercy, but far away and unreachable. I remained in an embrace with that pile of strong and relaxed muscles and I continued to say to myself that, like that, with my eyes closed, leaning against him, without speaking, in spite of everything, in spite of your compassion, perhaps life was not one constant, painful separation. A sweet but determined movement opened my arms and I saw him, my sweet nameless destiny, standing in front of me, ready to leave. I did not ask him for an explanation because none was necessary. His embrace, his closeness, had been momentary. They had nothing to do with my plans to fit into life once and for all. They had nothing to do with my intention to relax, like that, embracing him and awaiting death. The hours of the night in which a man embraces a woman ended, the moment to leave, to disappear without a trace into the night, arrived.

I returned to my own place, walking barefoot on the humid sand through the nighttime darkness. I reached my father's small, dilapidated theatre and there I saw him, with all his strength worn away, always at the point of collapse, on the shoddy, extravagantly lit stage, cracking a whip in the air as if he were threatening or chastising destiny so that it would award him the dramatic function that seemed to be eternally unattainable. I don't know if he was waiting for a miracle. He owned that run-down theatre, that building, that shell, but he would never have enough money to put on a play. I had grown up listening to his shouts and his cracking of the whip in the air. Without actors, without a script, without equipment. His only employee was a bland young girl who wasn't quite fat, with permanently wet, fat lips, half open to show several broad, widely-spaced teeth. Dressed in a type of clown suit with a white background and enormous red dots, with a straw hat, like that of a school girl, with two ribbons hanging from the rear of the brim. From time to time some members of the public would appear. The idiot would collect the entrance fee of ten centavos per person. Then my father's fury would increase. He had managed to get six, ten, twenty people ready to view what he would present to them, he had managed to collect a few miserable reales, but he had nothing to show them. Unwilling to admit his failure, he cracked his whip sharply in the air and from the stage he shouted at the girl collecting the reales with her drooling smile: "Idiot! Idiot! It's all your fault! Today will be another disaster, all because of you!" I heard his shouts without paying him any attention, knowing that the function would end without beginning, when the audience got bored with his shouts and the cracking of the whip in the air and would begin to get up and collect their reales from the hands of the smiling idiot. I carried on walking and took myself off to a kiosk where I ordered, with a triumphant air, a cup of hot chocolate. They served me the chocolate in a type of deep, small, cardboard tray and I did not complain. It was already late --nine o'clock at night--, and to procure service of that nature in a village almost totally asleep, was a privilege. We lived on the second floor, in a blackish and dirty pigeon loft, dark for lack of electric light or because my mother simply liked living like that. She was waiting for me with an attitude close to recriminatory: "You know that here, in this house, dinner is at seven on the dot". Inexplicably, I felt detached from the family yoke, I felt independent. I felt as though I had thrown, through a non-existent window, a sack bursting with guilt. Knowing that she was looking at me, I put a cynical smile on my face and said to her, while drinking from the tray of hot chocolate: "I know".

... AND THERE WAS LIGHT

A table. Two chairs. A café, a run-down café. A counter at the back. A waiter with a quite wet and fairly dirty apron and cap. The back of the café is desolate. A charged, dense, hot atmosphere, without a breeze. Sticky sweat on his forehead. The sleeves of his shirt rolled up nearly to his elbow. A rather pale arm. A clenched hand, in motion. In his hand, a cloth that circles and circles and circles tightly on the counter: the greasy stickiness must be eliminated from the counter. Thick, heavy flies, as if suffering from a pregnancy far longer than nine months. Their heavy stomachs cause them to fly low, low, slow, slow in the dense air. The automatic, mechanical movement of the hand cleaning. The waiter, his soul gone, continues bent over the counter. His gaze lost in an undefined point on the ground. Pale eyes that no longer even have the dullness of the insipid. Pale eyes that don't even contain the emptiness of absence. Gaze lost in some indefinite point on the ground. White hand, sometimes reddened by the soap and the pressure of the cloth. Slightly greying head of hair, empty of thought, in which perhaps some vague memory is housed. Eternal destiny? Punishment? Restitution?

In the front part of the run-down café an enormous
canopy provides shade for a group of tables. All arranged,
all clean, all empty. No, not all. All, except for one. A small,
round, iron table with two chairs. Two old men. Flabby skin.
Almost naked bodies covered by a loin cloth that made me
think of Gandhi. Long hair, aged bodies. These are the only
features they have in common. Are they judges? They are
having wine or something that looks like Benedictine or
Benedictine and brandy. Small, little plates which are now
empty which probably contained a salad with roquefort
cheese. Half-full glasses. Golden liquor, the shine of honey,
lifted from time to time by four fingers placed on the glass.

I walk up and down the sidewalk. A dense sun that
does not burn but instead turns one as sticky as molasses.
I look at the table from the sidewalk. The street separates
us. From time to time I rest my gaze on the occupied table.
A white haired old man with long, white hair and a long,
white beard. His chest, his shoulders, his arms, his back, his
thighs, his legs, his feet all naked. Flabby flesh. Hard bones,
untouched by Time. A serene, almost indifferent look, that
of a business Man that is about to close a deal in which the
most important element is to savour a glass of wine. His
hand, resting on the glass. A lowered gaze, not of humility,
but lightly meditative, like that of someone on the point of
weighing up a proposition that is made to him. A thousand
year-old, flabby heap, playing with a glass of wine. The
relaxed attitude of a listener.

The heavy, airless atmosphere brings me the persuasive
voice of the speaker. A thousand year-old man. Long black
hair. A Gandhi-type loin cloth. Half-naked, flabby body. A
purplish colour, with a yellowish tinge. A purplish colour
with a subtle yellowish tinge. The white of his eyes yellowed
with sharp yellow, like mustard. The dark pupil, bright,
sparkling, as if wounded by the reflections of a burning sun.
I know that if he were to look at me, he would completely

and absolutely dominate me. I know that I would stay static, rigid, immobile, locked in my hardening skin.

I know that no-one will notice me and I continue my slow, monotonous, heavy walk. With contained impatience, with contained curiosity, with contained anguish. I could give my anguish, my curiosity, my impatience, free reign. But, would that change my destiny? I ought only to walk about, waiting, as if in a maternity ward where children are manufactured, for my newly-born destiny to be manufactured. The judges --one active, the talker, the other passive, the listener-- continue the transaction without me. Perhaps they are negotiating my destiny, like great powers negotiate the destiny of some nation that has no voice nor vote in the deal.

I wait. I wait and remember. Should I intervene? I wait. I wait and remember. My ancestral learning tells me that I should run from the thousand year-old man with his burning gaze. In the History that deals with these questions, he is called cruel, capricious, active king of a torture chamber. What do I know about him? I know him as persuasive, drinking wine. The other one... the other one... I have spoken to him many times. Or rather, I should say, I have monologized with him through those formulas that have been invented so that we can address ourselves to him, and with many others that I myself invented. About this one, the History that deals with those things says that he is good, just and that he cares for us. How do I know him? I know that he handed over his son so that they could murder him. I know that he said that this was in order to save us. But it is said that very few were saved. How do I know him? When I do good, the thorns of pain gnaw, in payment, at my insides. I tried to create and my hands rotted and my works turned to dust. When I go to my brothers so that they can see me, their eyeless faces do not see me.

Eternal destiny? The next life? Hope? In that dense

atmosphere a type of bolt fell and there was light. Eternal destiny? The next life? Hope? For what? I made out an alleyway between two tall, worn-out buildings. I walked into it. For the first time I felt myself filled with a gigantic, herculean strength, capable of supporting a destiny that for the first time was mine. I felt huge in an infinitesimally small world. I entered a narrow, tortuous existence. Decidedly, fortunately, short. There, behind, remained the two thousand-year old men. Listening. Persuading. I tried to hold my gaze on them but I only saw the honey coloured shine of a glass of wine.

THE BATHERS

All this is said to have occurred on the Riviera or in some place like that.

A group of excursionists or perhaps just a collection of samples. Samples of men and samples of women. The virgin nun is there and the good workman is there. The healthy workman, the boring workman who does not raise his imagination nor causes it to take flight in others. In his little metal box is his sandwich, an apple and a thermos. Oh! How boring it is to watch a workman eat his lunch! But here all of that was left behind. We are on the Riviera and the nun abandoned her habit although she still seems to be wearing it and the workman abandoned his hardhat, his big boots and his lunch box. They bathe in bathing suits between fine sand and salty water. This continues for days and days. The excursionists bathe, the salty water, the half-strength sun, that neither burns nor cools, as if it had been graded. The bathers go and come, the bathers come and go. One day, one of them says, without speaking, because they don't speak as we would speak, but he says that the nun is getting married to the boring workman who is so boring. The nun abandoned her habit although she still seems to be wearing it.

The nun was on a stone patio with a stone well in the

centre and many flower boxes and many flowers and a great deal of pleasant humidity. Someone begins talking, (someone who, to hide himself, would even say that he was Don Juan), but knows that there is no evidence of identity and there is not the remote possibility that they would believe this and omits any introduction. He walks up to her as if the nun, next to the well, were waiting for this and, without more ado, he asks her for a kiss. It is possible that he may have asked her in another language to conceal all of this a little. Because saying it in another language may remove some of its seriousness. The nun is not offended and in the fear of her surprise, she is a little flattered. The nun did not respond in another language but spoke something that seemed to me to be a code: "The alabasters are doomed".

I started thinking about whether she wanted to say alabasters or albatrosses and I thought that in either case, that didn't make sense. And even without making sense, I understood perfectly. Because to a good understander, nonsense suffices. Because the reasons are so obvious that not even if they are said in another language could they be misunderstood. "Yes," I replied, "I have heard that bit about hell on other occasions" and I didn't tell her that I had seen hell in a movie about Goethe's *Faust* with all the music by Gounod. I didn't tell her that the voice of Gino Mattera playing Faust had moved me, nor did I tell her that it had seemed insulting to me that people had been sent to hell for things in which free will had hardly played a part while nature's errors indeed had. I'm not saying mistakes made by God so that Diderot shouldn't say that if God exists he has to be perfect and that if he makes mistakes it is because he does not exist. All of this deviation from the scene of the well and the garden is incongruent. Or perhaps it is utterly congruent.

The nun answered: "No. They don't send them --the

alabasters-- to hell. They hang them from that tower". A tall, very tall tower of the kind that corresponds to a phallic symbol or which is like the one in one of the courtyards of the University at Albany. "And they leave them like that, hanging from their hands, from the top of the tower, always flapping in the wind".

I was surprised by this oh-so strange information about which I knew nothing. I thought to myself that things from the other world will always be an unknown to me. When the nun mentioned the punishment she immediately felt free of it. She said to me, awaiting a contradiction with delight: "Let's get out of here". I insisted to her: "I want to see your house. Let's go in. Are you scared of me or are you scared of yourself?" With a smile of still to be achieved accomplishments: "I'm afraid of myself".

The house was old, with old furniture. A pristinely clean wooden floor, full of splinters. It was a house in which silly Pepita Jiménez would not get bored. But this nun, full of unmet desires, would vegetate in it. Her husband's rough boots, his hardhat, his lunch box and his quiet and so unimaginative goodness would only serve to kill her with boredom.

Upon entering the house, the habit which the nun no longer wore, ceased to be apparent. She sat down with a contented and satisfied happiness in a wicker armchair. I knelt before her and began beating my head against her left breast. While she suckled me as if I were a calf or a small deer, the transformation became complete. The voices of other times converged in her voice, in her laugh, the other laugh, in her giving, the other giving. I turned to confront the past and I drank it while at ease.

This is as much as is told about the bathers on the Riviera or from another place that resembles it. Sometimes they speak of the group of excursionists with their gaze lost in the distance, their automatic movements that do not respond to specific orders from the brain.

They speak of their eternal and useless mission to bathe in the sea and to drench themselves in sand. Nothing is known about the nun and no-one asks after her. She has probably married the workman bather but she has ceased to be a bather and to belong to the group even though she may be with them and she may bathe. She no longer has a fixed gaze. The shadow of her habit has now been lost forever.

They say that one day they saw her knitting on a bench on the beach. Her hair, slightly reddish, blowing in the wind. Withdrawn into herself, her gaze lost in the iodine air of the beach. An independent limb, separate from the clan of automatons that do not communicate.

IN THE LAND OF ICE

A place with no name, with no geographical record. A crowd of people. Men, women of twenty five to thirty years of age. A gigantic monster, like a huge prehistoric animal, begins to lift enormous rocks from the ground, gripping them between its jaws and throwing them to the ground in a fury, smashing them to smithereens. Another animal of the same type, two. Maybe thirty or forty metres high. In the shape of a dinosaur. Skin covered in hair. Long hair like that of some strange and diabolical dog. Laughter is heard which, to my surprise, came from me. One by one hundreds of heads turn around, hundreds of gazes. It was stupid to have laughed. I feel the humiliation of someone who has been foolish before others. Without understanding the situation. The focus of dismissive gazes. Their looks are frozen on me. And me in a place of which I had been unaware until that moment. A place that smells of the Arctic, of seals, of brine. Sea, boat, land, ice. Ice in my footsteps, cold in my hands. Embarrassment, looks. A rarefied air. I am petrified in the instant in which I am aware of myself. Of the others. Of that cold, strange, unknown, briny place. I need to flee that instant frozen in Time. From those gazes that I feel stuck to my skin, to my nakedness, to my embarrassment. I start smiling and I slowly point with my finger to a thick glass wall, incredibly tall and thick. My gaze takes in the roundness of the wall. A wall that surrounds and encloses. My finger points towards two monsters and I explain: "The fictional monsters, created by the movies, for the movies, make you laugh". The reproachful looks that moments before had crossed my skin, were transformed into looks of surprise. A dark youth, with a skin of light cinnamon, dark eyes, black hair, thin. Black trousers, a worn-out and dirty leather belt, a turtle-neck sweater, black. A knitted cap, black. An air of a merchant marine. He looked at me as if he could not believe my ignorance: "These are not fictional monsters".

Men and women of twenty five to thirty years old. Each independent and, at the same time, united by a mission that no-one is able to comprehend. A fateful mission of which no-one is aware. They all approach the sea, the quay, amid a laughter and an eagerness that is devoid of happiness. Everything smells of death, of death as we know it here. Of a death where we ask ourselves what does one feel when one ceases to feel. When flesh decays and the heart doesn't beat and our lungs don't work and we're inside, locked into a box, covered by earth. When we ask ourselves what the worms that devour our toes will be like.

I follow the crowd, I walk up to the edge. There is a boat that is more like one of Columbus's ships. In it, the master will experience the infinite pleasure of a small journey. Of a journey that will last one to ten minutes. The ship will turn around in a complete circle. The master will be accompanied by a few privileged people. She was next to the master. The only person I recognised. The only person who comes from the other, the same world I come from. The master seems to possess her. They seem to be joined by a fateful ceremony that must inevitably be celebrated. A ceremony that they do not quite understand.

The master, enjoying himself with the briny water that

splashes him, smiles with a mouth in which his teeth don't seem to fit very well. He appears to be about forty five years old. His skin is sunburnt and greasy. Brown hair, greasy. A white, linen shirt, clean. While he chats to a young woman that he has at his side and who seems to be his secretary, he grabs my acquaintance round the waist with his enormous hands, and sits her down on his lap. She smiles. A little bothered, but submissive. Joined to him by the fateful ceremony that will, inevitably, take place. The launch's motor is already running. Those people that have remained on the quay laugh happily. Satisfied, contented, by the master's journey with his companions. Hundreds of arms are raised in farewell. The rejoicing increases when one of them makes out a shield that the ship has near its prow. "It's the emblem of León", someone says. "It's a Spanish ship". And the delight increases. In this nameless land with no record there is a ship of known origin. This land full of people of no known origin, with no destiny, possesses an identifiable object. The recognisable girl. The ship turning in a circle. The same beautiful face, the same smile. She does not seem to know me. She does not seem to attribute importance to my presence there. Annoyed, sitting on the master's lap, but submissive. Waiting for the big ceremony that will inevitably be celebrated. She gets up carefully so as not to offend the master and sits down next to him. I stop following with my eyes, the route taken by the ship. I detach the movement of the ship turning in a circle from my eyes. The fatefully happy faces that surround me are erased. The master's pleasure upon feeling his face splashed with briny water is erased. I turn on my heels slowly and begin to watch the monsters behind the glass wall. For the first time I try to explain the presence of these abominable beings to myself. Their reality. Their function. Their importance. I did not find a logical answer. Only I represented a reality. Everything else, even if it was in front of me, escaped from me into a world of dreams, a world of nightmares. I was real. The woman I recognised <u>had</u> to be real. She had always been so. But I tried to call her and she did not seem to recognise me. I had the feeling that perhaps the master would present one of those beings before the monsters and that this ritual could result in a horrible and useless tragedy. Why die in such a stupid manner? I tried to warn the woman I recognised. I headed for the ship. The passengers were already disembarking. The woman I knew was still at the master's side as if she carried an invisible and inevitable destiny.

They started walking along a path opened between the frozen and smooth ground. The master and my acquaintance walked in the midst of the crowd. He, guiding. I limited myself to following that mass of people. I had decided to reach my acquaintance, in some way, and to try and wake her from that illogical submissiveness. To try and pull from her that so useless and so tragic destiny by which she felt trapped without seeming to have the will to rid herself of it. The master's paws squeezed her shoulder. I tried to get closer. I had to tell her that sacrifice is for nothing and death, something so stupid. Why not try to escape? Why not exercise your will? Why not offer resistance? It seemed to me that my acquaintance let herself be led onwards just to get it over with. To end it once and for all and then to be free. But, how does one get out of this? How does one get out of a useless death?

The monsters with their long, white hair had remained behind. They seemed powerful, like gods. Repulsive, cruel, inescapable gods. Gods that had delegated to the master the task of choosing their victims to be offered to them as sacrifices. Gods unconcerned with the pain and the deaths and the fear of the people. Gods locked into their glass urn dedicated to their rages and their games.

What were these people who walk like this, in a crowd,

looking for? What were they looking for, led --although not ostensibly so-- by the master? A place to carry out the sacrifice? A place high up in that mountain that we had before us where the monsters could enjoy themselves like that, high up, like that, masters of nature, where they could frolic before a useless death? Why die? Death is so stupid! I tried to warn my acquaintance. I had to urge her to escape. The master seemed implacable, inescapable. But, how could it be possible that she didn't at least try to escape? With this anguish I worked my way into the crowd. We were heading up hill. The ice made me slip and when I thought that I might fall into the abyss, someone held me by my arms and attached me to the group once more. She was a militia woman dressed in an olive green uniform. With a rifle on her shoulder. Acting like a night watchman or a jailer responsible for seeing that no prisoners escape. I moved into the centre of the crowd. In vain I searched for the master and for my acquaintance. I felt myself filled by that anguish that possesses us when we are helpless. I was filled with the anguish produced by impotence. I heard the powerful voice of another woman with a rifle ordering us to take off our shoes. I knew that I would not be able to walk for very long on the ice without my feet freezing. My interior anguish became desperation and I started to run. I saw a type of many-storied tower and headed for it. It was made of logs stripped of their bark. Of thick, damp logs, one on top of the other. Inside, one empty room on top of the next. Joining the rooms, an inner, vertical staircase. Upon reaching the doorway to the tower, I saw myself immersed in another crowd. They were all senior citizens, old people that I looked at all together, without stopping to look at any one. I think they were women. Old women, dishevelled, walking like tired automatons, subjected to an invisible and inescapable force that made them climb the tower, walk about each empty room and go down again.

Without knowing how I got there, I found myself in one of the unfurnished rooms that would have been on the second or third floor. Behind me I heard a booming voice shout: "Ana! Ana Mar!". I joined in too: "Ana! Ana Mar!" I realised then that both of us were calling my acquaintance by a name that was not hers but which she would respond to, if she were there, upon hearing it called.

Amongst that human load, amongst those remains full of pain, of sadness and of grief, I found my aunt Ana. Full of age and on the verge of collapse she said to me: "You called me. At last someone has called me. If you trust in God, someone will call you". Without being aware of truth's brutal cruelty, I said to her: "I am calling Ana Mar", and I stressed the surname. My aunt lowered her eyes, frowned slightly and renewed, with a tired step, the march of the eternal and repeated journey.

I made an effort to make her see that I was still concerned for her: "How are you, Aunt? She hardly answered me and carried on walking. I noticed then that her husband wasn't with her. My initial intention was to ask after him, but I refrained from doing so. I didn't want to find out about deaths or prisons or enslavements. I imagined him seated on an earthen floor, with all the failure of his senility, starving and humiliated in some concentration camp. I did not halt my aunt in her march. I did not want to hear anything. I tried to make my way through the crowd. Carrying with me a profound anguish I shouted: "Ana! Ana Mar!".

CAPTAIN TOAD

Five years old. Plaits. Shy, quiet and serious. Halfway through the kitchen door, I approach Captain Toad from a long way off. Half a step higher than the rest of the house, this room, full of pots and pans and grills, is my watchtower from where I can observe --or spy?-- on the king of the courtyard. Captain Toad, on guard in the drain, does not allow any insect to enter. All formally dressed in green, croak, croak, croaks Captain Toad. An old toad who moves slowly but who gets around with his eyes and inspects everything from the four corners. The door is half open. I lean a little way out to approach Captain Toad from a long way off. My heart gives little jumps and the cold licks my fingers and the soles of my feet. My aunts in the sitting room, in the Grown-ups' world, carry out their chores. I approach Captain Toad from a long way off. One of my eyebrows emerges, half my face emerges and my small hand loses itself in the doorway. What mystery and what fear one feels in the world of the king of the courtyard! All formally dressed in green, croak, croak, croaks Captain Toad. My heart jumps like a ram, my thoughts cloud over and the exact and enormous words that I have to announce to the Grown-ups so that they throw Captain Toad out of the courtyard escape me: "The Captain is... is powerful and... and frightening... and is ugly... and is the boss of everything".

Five years old. Quiet, shy and serious. The passing of Time lost in the recesses of my subconsciousness. Somewhat removed from living. The passing of Time is playtime and lunchtime and bedtime. The passing of a lot of time is Christmas and my birthday. It is nighttime and being afraid of the dark. It is daytime and being afraid of Captain Toad. It is talking to the Grown-ups with a strength that becomes ice flakes and snowflakes. It is saying that Captain Toad is powerful and ugly and is the boss of everything and... it is having to keep watching him and spying on him from the room full of pots and pans and grills.

Five years old. Shy, quiet and serious. Collecting bits of news that I hear and that is not told directly to me. The neighbours have moved and have left behind... toys! I slip into the house right next to mine. So much mystery in an empty house! So many hidden treasures! Papers in the sitting room. Papers in the dining room and in the hallways. The toys... there are no toys, but what mystery and what adventure! I have to see everything, I must inspect everything, searching for the footprints and the marks of those who have left. The rooms hold something so intimate that I am scared to enter. In the courtyard the flowers of those who have left are still growing. In the flowerpots they left the movement of their hands during mornings of caring and watering. Papers on the floor. Particles of dust piling up. Everything left behind on the floor. Sticking out from amongst piles and piles is a little snout. It's a small piece of wood with a duck painted on it. Only the neck and the head in profile and one eye and half of the beak. Had it been waiting for me? Crouched down, I examined it. Slowly I get up and, without knowing it, clasp the duck to my chest. The voices of the Grown-ups jump the boundary wall. It's lunchtime. A plate of lentils or beans and meat and potatoes. It's time to make the effort to leave one's toys and to sit down and eat. I leave in a hurry and in silence. With little trots of my patent leather shoes. Patent leather with laces. In my hands, clasped to my chest, a recently saved friend. I reached the door and before me stretched the porch and the stairs and Calixto García Street. To travel quickly from the porch of the people who have left to mine, I crossed over through the bars of the common railing. How should I explain my acquisition? "Good and decent little girls do not go to strange houses nor do they take things even if these have been abandoned". Would they say that to me? With enormous indifference I showed them the painted head of the duck. No comments were made and I seated it at the table, at my side. A name, a name for my recently saved friend. Either I didn't find one or I don't remember it. An eagerness not to loose it or to have it with me wherever I went made me trace the duck's outline with pencil on pieces of white paper. The many pencil reproductions did not make me feel that my riches where increasing. One day, that I may not remember out of disloyalty, I lost the piece of wood.

The Grown-ups say that we have new neighbours. They are mulattos and the father is a lawyer and the uncle a doctor. There are five children and amongst them there is a little girl older than I am. The day of the move arrived and my heart began giving little jumps and the same cold as always licked my hands and the soles of my feet. How does one make friends with new children? I didn't even meet the others, the ones who left. I heard noises and voices outside and I dared to go out. I went up to the small railing. Each hand clutching a bar and my head stuck through them. A girl quite a bit bigger than me skated on the porch. Her back exposed and her red dress torn and unbuttoned at the back. My hands held on tightly to the bars and when the girl, in an involuntary movement of the roller-skate, approached me, I said to her: "Here we have a toad called Captain". The expected surprise did not materialise. She made a gesture of indifference and lost herself in the depths of the house and of the other voices.

Darkness in silence. Lips sealed on the infinite and enormous mouth of Time, of the hours, of the late hours of night. A small hand resting on one side of the white, very white sheet. The other, under the pillow, as if wanting to grab hold of a plait ending in half untied ribbon that was unravelling. The ceiling divided into pieces, made into squares, a grid map copying the squares of the rectangular mosquito netting. Paint, whitewashed plaster, bricks, cement: a wall. Me, without touching it, perpendicular to it, on my back. The edges of the ceiling hurrying to die in angles. Three angles in each corner. One, two, three... four corners. The silence neither comes nor goes. It remains static, in a stillness that one feels. Five, ten, fifteen minutes, half an hour. Everyone is asleep and the silence feels safe, powerful, reigning in the solitude with a force that cannot be seen, nor touched, nor brushed against, but which is there. The darkness has drained away to the outside, towards the courtyard, towards the plants, towards the kitchen and the stove. Towards the spaces between the stars and the moon. The white edges of the white sheet begin being born, to sprout, to make themselves visible. An awareness of the reclining body, resting on the sheets and, at the same time, with a kind of tension in its throat. A tension that turns to little rivers of cold to enter the chest and to explore there the layers of the heart. A tension that turns into sweat to explore the palms of the hands. A tension that becomes a light tickling to explore the soles of the feet and to make the tarsus move like two small fans. The soft, white bed and the tight tendons, pulling. A voiceless time, a time to enter another world where others do not go. The paint from edge to edge which wants to be the sun and be yellow like the yellow of a chicken and shine and be smooth and strong. Majestic paint that covers the wall. A wall painted with oils that I look at from my horizontal position. I widen a little the angle of my vision and I find myself face to face with quadrilateral shadows that seem to be moving, getting into a position from which to fall on me. I fix my gaze on them, daring them, awaiting a fall that I know will not take place. My attention is drawn towards the wall painted in oil paint. The layers of paint, little by little, with the tick-tock steps of a watch, roll themselves up, like a parchment. After rolling up, they unroll themselves and stretch themselves once more. A hole suddenly appears without there having been an explosion, without being the result nor the consequence of anything. There are no movements, there is no suddenness. It appears as if born in the night, of the night, for the night. Behind where the paint and the layer of plaster had been, bricks begin appearing, like teeth lying down. From between the cement that borders each brick, long nails stuck to a toad's fingers come through. Claws trapped, immobile, in the wall. Claws equidistant to the skin of a stomach in the shape of a dickie worn under a tailcoat. A stomach of silk or of wet satin, gelatinous, slippery. White eyes, bulging balloons, stuck to the wall from which they seem to stick out without moving. My legs have been stuffed with icicles. And my fingers, the tips of my fingers, with tiny hailstones. A weakness that more than anything is like whip lashes of absence surrounds the edges of my eyes and loses itself in my forehead. Everything begins to disappear and I submerge myself in unconsciousness.

Day made of clarity has filled the room. I opened my eyes to a light room, without mysteries, without dense areas, without silences. I look at the wall now foreign to me. Empty of any enthusiasm although perhaps with a little embarrassment. As if I were presenting myself before a mute witness to my fear, to my feelings of cold, to my sweats, to my tensions. Like you would look at someone to whom you have made an involuntary confession. I left my room to begin measuring it all. To start to measure the reality reduced by the light of day.

WHEN THE STILLNESS COMES ALIVE

It is four in the afternoon. Time sets the clock. The wind, an ethereal, flexible and strong serpent, smashes itself into tiny pieces against the façades of buildings. Exterior Time moves in a straight line, progressing towards the future. Interior Time wanders the crannies of my mind and slows down, speeds up or stops. The torpor of a light sleep falls spontaneously and slowly over each eye muscle. My leaden sight slowly stops moving, focusing on nothing. Now blurry, it hangs in the atmosphere dancing a motionless dance. The slow heaviness of sleep separates itself from me, step by step. I begin to disappear and, with the incorporeity of ether, I penetrate and become absorbed into the motionless matter of things and pieces of furniture and tables... the table... I am absorbed into the spinning and subatomic world of neutrons and protons. With my arms wide and my hands clutching the light, indivisible particles, I float, forming rings in a world without gravity, with the slow step of a slow-motion camera. "Courage, courage, the platter is broken... the little birds sing..." "How much will you give me, sailor, if I get you out of the water, yes, yes... If I get you out of the waaterrr..." A small, muffled voice that sings without hearing itself singing rhymes.

A garden of echoes. The vibrating corner of a train that shakes and pulls me. In the compartment I feel the unvarying force of the wheel which devours stretch after stretch after stretch, all equal. A tan uniform. The shadow of a dress. An officer who sits next to someone. A smile. They take each other's hand. Their fingers entwine without squeezing. They look at one another. An uncomplicated look without roots, of youth that has not suffered. The train continues to cover distance. The black letters on page 75 begin disappearing. My fingers loosen their grip, the book falls onto my lap. Tall grass, short grass, trees and fences.

I'm gliding, towards the shores of the pearl Island. I want to arrive now, in my thirties, and I arrive as an adolescent wearing a cotton dress and a red raincoat. I arrive in torrential rain on a day in which I catch buses and walk along San Rafael Street. A student's purse: a sandwich, a "flying saucer" sandwich. I arrive on a day during which I go to the Cathedral and catch buses and walk along San Rafael Street. The Chinese Quarter draws closer and I am imbued with mystery and fear. Slices of glazed pumpkin, longed for in the province of Oriente: a little packet, a little paper bag, one, two... fifteen centavos. The humid streets and the now dry sky put me in a good mood while walking along San Rafael Street. During the repeated movement of my hand from the paper bag to my mouth, I pause. A tan dress with white checks. A dress with tan and white checks. The University... the tan dress. The new dress in classes. No money. A tan dress with white checks. A white and tan checked dress in the University. The street disappears and I sink into the freshness of the air conditioning. The store, El Encanto, expensive and good. No money. A checked dress for the University. Credit: the manager. My aunt from the Oriente Province will pay for it. No money. The tan dress. My aunt from Oriente, in the Oriente agency, will pay for it. Sealed box, with a handle, like cups have. Inside, my tan dress for the University. I am filled with fear... or is it guilt? My aunt from Oriente, who buys nothing for herself, will pay for my dress for the University.

I want to go to my Island of Oriente, of Vedado neighbourhood, of Havana, in my thirties and I arrive as an adolescent, on a day marked by torrential rain. Ethereal, I slip into the matter. Into the matter of tables and thick planks. Into the matter of spinning subatomic particles, of neutrons and protons. Ethereal, I cannot reach my Island which no longer exists. My Island of Oriente and of Vedado and of Havana. Because I know that it is another island and I haven't seen it like this: broken. And without having seen it I cannot arrive there in my ethereal state, in my state of light sleep. I vaporise myself and I want to arrive in my thirties but I arrive as an adolescent and I go for a stroll around my unaltered Island which I have never seen broken. I see my Island without pain and without the blood it bathes itself in and without hunger. Without hatred, without torture and without torn baby clothes. My soul stretches to reach its pain, mine. And I bring it back to myself through comments and words. Through the pain of others that shreds to pieces in broken hearts. And I bring it back to myself in a newspaper clipping which mentions, incidentally, that twenty people died trying to escape. I vaporise myself and I glide, towards the shores, towards my pearl Island. I extend myself to feel her pain, my pain, on my lips. And I arrive as an adolescent, on a day marked by torrential rain and I walk along San Rafael Street.

Ten past four in the afternoon. The postman arrives. Time sets the clock.

Note
The author left Cuba in 1957

CAIMANERA

To live is to dissolve. I dissolve myself, you dissolve yourself. But even worse: you-I-we dissolve ourselves. He dissolved himself in death. She lives disconnected, without ties, in the unlife, stuck to a headache, to an attack of rheumatism.

We draw closer to the ghost village. We cannot distinguish anything in the distance. We sense it. Our intuition sharpens itself on the horizon and brings to it a prophetic atmosphere, a charged, drivelling atmosphere. We cannot see the village, we will never see it, but we know that we have arrived. We also know that we are, exactly, on a south-east point of the Island, near the bay. An isolated fishing village, an island on another island.

We knew that we had arrived because we were in my home. The temperature became cooler, as if to relieve us, for a moment, from the feeling of death. My father arrived bringing paper bags and boxes of supplies, as if all that had no purpose. It was not our sustenance. It did not matter who they were for. They were supplies for the house. My mother was there, in that darkened room, nibbling at some flower of death.

They were young, almost as young as you and I. You, standing by my mother's bed, were waiting, with a tragic passion, for something that escaped my understanding.

With your head held high, your gaze led you to his figure. Taking packets out of the paper bags. Taking out cans of food. Taking out all that as if it were his only reason for living. Your tragic, intense gaze filled the silence of the afternoon. You recognised him. You were waiting for him. You had never seen him but you recognised him as you would recognise those beings who have to be recognised. You wandered endlessly through the house with a tragic tread that was heavy but restless at the same time. With that painful agitation that beasts in cages in the circus or in the zoo have.

He allowed himself to be recognised by you without, at the same time, recognising you himself. He was not destined to recognise anyone. His feet never touched the ground and only mad butterflies made their home in his mind. Once I envied him. On another occasion I despised him. He was designed so that pain could not touch him. I envied that wall of obliviousness that protected him. I believed that he did not have the right to a place at the table, a bowl of soup, or beans, or rice. I believed that he was obliged never to die so as not to weigh on people's consciences. And, little by little, I began to despise him because a man without pain is a man without dignity. It hurt me that he was not ridiculous so that I could laugh at him. He simply <u>was not</u>. Quite simply, his bread never turned sour in his mouth, and knots never formed in his throat. One day my mother said that he had cried. And I asked myself if he would cry like a woman or like a little girl or like a little boy. "Yes? He cried?" And I nodded my head several times without knowing myself how to interpret my gesture.

My father allowed you to recognise him and wandered the house speaking to you in corners in a low voice. And you recognised him and he could only allow himself to be recognised. And you, if you moved away, you were back in front of him again and you allowed a love that tasted of death to escape. And he could only allow himself to be recognised.

At that precise moment the tragedy began. In her sick bed, tied to her life of death, she accused you of stealing her dignity. I felt the edge of the knife, the cold edge, searching for some place in my chest. I wanted to think, I wanted to meditate, I wanted to invent beautiful worlds and I could only tell her: "No, Mother, there is nothing. There isn't anything between them". Her fury in that miasma of death pained me because I understood that it wasn't the loss of my father that tormented her, but her loss. To suffer, to feel jealousy implies the existence of intense feelings. But here, in the prostrate wreckage, there was only a painfully ineffectual attempt to hold on to her dignity as a woman. It was all that was left to her. And I thought how we are moved to compassion over the poverty of a human being who treasures a pebble collected on some faraway beach and who clings to it as if it were the point that marked her identity, her homeland, her environment, her essence, her right to life.

At that precise moment the tragedy began. I had to talk to you on behalf of that woman, for her, for my mother. I would talk to you on her behalf. I would talk to you for my mother. I would talk to you for that woman. The strands of my thought crisscrossed and I saw life with its habitual pieces loose. Everything falls in the exact place where it does not fit. And those places that should be full remain, forever, condemned to emptiness, starving.

My proposition was simple: that you should go and live somewhere else. "After all, if you love each other, what better than an intimate place". You opened your arms in his direction, sending him your tragic look. "I can't do that. I would never see him again". I didn't stop to think that the town, Caimanera, did not exist. That we had never seen it. That all we had was that house to which he was eternally tied. I did not think that I had never found it strange that the town might not exist, nor that it would be possible to bring supplies from a town that did not exist.

We had to get out of that place. You. Me. You-me-we dissolved ourselves, but it was essential that we speak. It was essential that we prevent all of that. In the name of death. In her name. In the name of that woman. In the name of my mother.

We left. We went to a village that wasn't that one because in that one there was no room for anyone's presence. We went to a village where the sun was Spanish. And the streets were Spanish. And the trees too. I recognised my car and was not surprised by the fact that it shouldn't be there. Space did not exist and distance devoured itself.

I let you drive. I don't know why you wanted to. I don't know myself why I did not want to drive. You drove very seriously and very badly. The car seemed like one of those machines from hell that you find in carnival celebrations. Your seriousness alarmed me. I was frightened that you wouldn't understand that at that rate we would finish off the village. You stopped. I tried a joke that left a bitter taste in me and that you would not catch. "In another house... you two... more intimacy". I honestly spoke with faith, believing in the effect my words would have. I couldn't finish. Your arms stretched out into infinity. Your tragic look extended to the horizon. "I can't do that. I would never see him again".

And at that precise moment the tragedy began.

HYDRA

It is odd that the man should be half wood. Poseidon. He remained between the rocks. I dived two, three times and there he stayed. The Laughing Buddha, half of iron. "I wasn't a siren any more. I went out into the world and all the Cro-Magnons were waiting for me. In giving, I looked ridiculous because they sucked at me like a whirlwind. They sucked me in by the index finger and my reflection stayed hanging in any agora". Small boats. Big boats. "The half iron-stone-wood Neptune saw me without having to focus". Serene. He was sitting beneath an awning. For him the most innocent thing: a stone from the bottom of the sea. We're in Hydra.

-- "I brought you a stone from the bottom of the sea. From the sea at Hydra."

-- "I'll put it on a chain". In Malaysia. When Poseidon-Laughing Buddha-stone-metal-wood Neptune is called B.J. (be-jay) he will carry it around his neck. His figure smiled --broken Apollo-- and all the rest: each Cro-Magnon in his cave. A thread broke. Another thread broke. All the threads broke. And all the Cro-Magnons broke too.

"I'm alone on an island full of Cro-Magnons". She is alone and knows it. She walks along the shore and clean water appears from between the stones. Solitude in the very line of the horizon. Solitude in a crevice in the rock where a crab moves backwards.

"I came from the sea". She came from the sea. A tunic down to her heels. Poseidon's lover, no, Neptune's lover, no, he's stone. She looks for the mother island. She looks for Sappho's throat. Sappho's vocal chords. Sappho's throat, broken. It's the VI Century before the invention of the Nazarene. It is the XX Century when they no longer invent anything.

"I came from the sea". She came from the sea. And in the friendly writing owl's eyes began to grow. She had read: <u>Come, I need you by my side</u>. And upon reading the cramped writing she made these words her own. "And I came from the sea". And she came from the sea. And from the friendly writing grew three prongs --not a trident-- and she began collecting drachmas.

--I care for you a great deal for one drachma. I love you a lot for three drachmas. You are my sister for five drachmas.

Upon hearing this she came from the sea. "I came from the sea". She tried to hear Sappho and the waves of the sea did not form her voice. Her heel-length skirts began to make marks on the sand. No blood came from any of the furrows. Her heel-length skirts absorbed all the water of the ocean without once retaining it. Perhaps the boy from the temple, the wise child, knows how to explain in all languages what solitude is. "And I came from the sea". She came from the sea and all the routes to the temple were closed. She turned back, dragging her feet over the sand and not once did blood spring from the furrows. There the writing was: <u>Come, I need you by my side</u>. She extended her arms to join in brotherhood with another human being. "I will be part of the wheel". She will be part of the wheel and will turn with all the Cro-Magnons in the world and the siren will die and the cold will leave her flesh. Owl's eyes and an echoing voice sprang from the friendly writing and she repeated: "You will be my sister for five drachmas".

She continued to drag her heel-length skirts and no blood sprang from the furrows of sand. Stuck to the coldness of the rocks, a crab marched backwards.

Heel-length tunic. She continued her march watched by the rocks, felt by the echo, intuited by the stones at the bottom of the sea. The rocks and the stones and the echo wanted to follow her but they were stuck to the centre of the earth and to the bottom of the sea and to the roots of the air. She retraced her steps and the owl's eyes stopped her and the voice of the echo said: "If you're going to the Nazarene it will cost you ten drachmas. I will be your sister for five drachmas and you can be just another Cro-Magnon for one drachma".

"But I didn't want to return to the sea". But she did not want to return to the sea and, always dragging her heel-length skirts, she went to the god Laughing-Buddha-Wood-Iron and she gave him a stone from the bottom of the sea. She moved away without blood springing from her footprints and she spoke to all the Cro-Magnons of the world in an unintelligible language. And all the Cro-Magnons spoke at the same time of the rise-fall, of the hamburger, of the three hijacked planes, of Nixon's nose, of six lira, four drachmas and an Alitalia waiting room. And she tried to explain: "I came from the sea to be just another Cro-Magnon". And the voice of the owl became enormous: "Show your drachmas".

She opened her hands filled with stones from the bottom of the sea. The owl absorbed all the Cro-Magnons. She hung them in her stomach. She prepared herself to dispense death. The heel-length skirts waited docilely on the sand.

"I have died a death from bloodless wounds".

She has died a death from bloodless wounds.

Greece
Summer '72

THE CIRCUS

He was backstage once more, standing before the mirror. Another performance. One more. Chaining one day to the next like a series of matinees so that the children could laugh because the clown tripped, because he slipped, because they threw water at him. So that the adults could laugh, all the while convincing themselves that their amusement was only a reflection of the children's happiness. And perhaps it was. But a reflection lacking in clarity. Their laughs seemed more like involuntary coughs. Without that explosive shout that the children's laughter contained. He had become accustomed to seeing himself in the flowers along the road, wild and bitter. In the abandonment of solitary rails. He never knew why they had castrated him. All he remembered was the smooth voice of the man who at times served as a link so that he could hold onto the group.

Over the liquor and the baked delicacies people talked about a cabaret with telephonic and pneumatic intercommunication. Later the irreplaceable need to define himself arrived, of knowing up to what point, at what point, he formed part of everyone else. "Egolatry", someone said. And he began drowning in the other voice that overcame his voice. He knew that his voice turned aside in the air like the smoke of Cain's lambs. And he was unable to convince anyone that they were not casting pearls before swine. But it was necessary to try. To fill the gap. To reach an agreement. Until another voice said: "Let him speak so we can see how far he goes". And then he touched his fragile voice, like a thread curled on a table under the gaze of that stuffed owl. Meekly he opened his legs. The dry and well-aimed blow separated him from himself and from the others. He walked in the night like a sick animal, living under the skin of the Father of the Six Characters, classified forever by one gesture. In his pocket he felt a list of books and saved forever the exact moment in which he handed over thirty pesos for cigarettes. A few steps to reach the corner. A beggar who is satisfied with two pesos. The bus, with a seven in front, like an opaque star. The streets had all been disordered and he wandered in the night, aimlessly. It didn't matter whether he reached Maipú Street, nor Corrientes Street, nor Lavalle Street, nor whether he went by Reloj Café. Nor whether he felt the death that one carries inside oneself. Walking without feeling one's steps. Seeing how the lines on one's hand erase themselves.

He had walked through many towns that left no history behind them. They only left a list of successive misunderstandings. Of exact estrangements. The impresario seemed grotesque to him. He was revolted by those chubby hands that constantly counted a wad of notes. To be a number in that sad farce which was destined to entertain others. To cover with reds and whites the deep lines that identified a sad face. To plaster a smile on with thick black outlines, always ready for two o'clock in the afternoon. The puppet show was always the most devastating. Manipulated like dead rags with others' voices. The tigers' voraciousness. The tamer's skill. And Maggie, always Maggie, with her monumental and greasy corpulence, who insisted that she had been a professor at Cologne University and who uttered unintelligible words like "Teutons" and for whom the elephants were always "pachyderms". She spoke of strange myths and she ordered everyone around with desperate gestures so that they would never approach that woman they called the Titan. Only Maggie mentioned the Titan. She said that the Titan had come from far away to wander with the circus. To be at the same time fixed and unchanged by the sea and by time, like those columns in Greece. She swore that to remove her from that isolation would be equivalent to killing her. The chubby dwarf always listened to Maggie with enormous eyes and everyone obeyed her without understanding her. For fear of having unstoppable curses flung at them. According to Maggie, everything came from classic balance. From not falling. From walking along that wire without the help of bars. Without safety nets. Always setting a higher goal. As if seeking the point at which one would meet death.

He had been walking that morning, some two kilometres in search of a flower. That was his routine. To slip between the curtains and to place a rose in an empty vase on the Titan's dressing table. Maggie was unaware of this. She would never know it. And he would never tell himself that it was a wasted ritual. Necessary only to recover the sensation of being alive.

That night, at eight, an important performance would begin. The tension could be felt in the atmosphere. The dwarves marched past with an unusual and a grotesque to-ing and fro-ing. Some of the group, with a solemn preoccupation reflected on their faces, approached Maggie. The scaffolding was damaged. It would be dangerous to walk the tight-rope. With a furious gesture, Maggie told them to leave. The performance had nothing to do with these details. It was all a question of keeping faith with the myth. Balance. Not falling.

He had finished washing the colours from his face and had wiped off his smile. He felt tense, invaded by an anguish that had overcome him and that formed something concrete and gloomy in his chest. He had to do something. He could not leave the Titan to face the danger on her own. He heard the drum rolls and he imagined her alone, walking towards her death. He quickly went out when he heard the crowd's astonished murmur. The rope, torn. The Titan, launched into the air, swinging in space like a pendulum. Something made her recover her equilibrium and she managed to slowly descend. As if obeying a release of tension, the clown ran to her and gave her his hand, unnecessarily, to help her descend the last section. As if obeying the call of a curse that was still to be carried out, that woman, created out of myths, fell heavily, deafly, onto the earthen floor. The audience remained motionless as if, out of her death, she had not allowed them to make a gesture of compassion.

Buenos Aires

July, 1973

THE TWO-HEADED MONSTER

The monster walked impatiently along Florida Street. Neither this one nor that one saw him. His hump lay quietly on his back. The two-headed monster had come to escape. And running away was not a part of his nature. But he was here to run away. He did not want to appear in *Curiosities of Nature* in a photo taken with excellent cameras which would not miss the most minute detail of his deformity. Someone said that it would be better to call it deviance and that all this was a real pity, but, on the other hand, one shouldn't kill the monsters. But all that was very annoying, even if they did spare him his life.

The deformity was on his back and he was taking a walk along Florida Street. He forgot that photographic cameras existed. He forgot about each and every one. Even those by Kodak and Minolta. His head ached, tucked into his right shoulder, and one day it began to bleed through the straps that imprisoned it. But all that was a deviation and a deformity and it was necessary to hide it for the good of humanity. For the good of our brothers. Of all our brothers who are full of normal deviations that do not need to be hidden. Deviations that should not be named if one does not wish to preach. But something makes it necessary to note that the most cruel deviation is carried by those who spare the life of monsters who will never cease to be, in their eyes, deformed and deviant.

It was difficult for the monster to walk along Florida Street with his head twisted over his shoulder, imprisoned. But when he saw the Ateneo Bookshop he managed to smile and when he saw a clothes store which used to get supplies from a large department store which no longer exists, he was able to smile. And he even believed and told himself, firmly, that with smiles --which were authentic-- everything could be wiped out, including any possible deviation. His self deception was authentic. And if he did not forget his pain, he did become accustomed to living with the pain. But it was all an annoyance without an end or a solution. And he was visited by the recurrent and obsessive image of a woman, dressed in grey gauze, beating on a wall, a wall made of wooden planks that rose in front of her to forever prevent her escape. And he realised, with the precision of Sherlock Holmes, that this was a symbol. This was inescapable oppression. And knowing this was meaningless because, while he smiled at the Ateneo Bookshop, the woman continued beating and the boards remained mute before the rain and before the sun and before the afternoon mist. He saw with complete clarity the painful mythological repetition. And then not having read Thomas Wolfe ceased to be of importance. And shortly thereafter the moment of truth arrived. And someone asked without cruelty, I don't know whether for classification or for clarification: "Tell me, do you have that deviation?" And of course the answer should have been, flatly, "No". But it was aggravating to live without authenticity and he replied with another question: "A confession... for what?" And in that question-answer was the true answer and the blood on his back became slightly visible. And this was like evidence or an identity card. There was no other option but to go through the business of having them spare him his life "despite everything". At that moment all attempts at explanation ceased because it is a sin to explain what is logical and what everyone should know: that God had forgotten to create him in his image and likeness or that nature had an urge to make mistakes and that now it was up to him to suffer the consequences of that mistake. Explanations were useless. It was useless to try to convince anyone that he had not chosen the materials from which he was made. He only made mention of one thing without intending that it should be an excuse. Only to reiterate, in order to show that oh-so definite and precise logic which no-one wished to see. The night was all light and shadow, in an interrupted sleep. The word "monster", made of letters like dry leaves, came loose from the ceiling to rain down on him. And he didn't dare scream because then everyone would know. However, the letters fell apart as they reached him, without touching him. It was like an echo of the whole of humanity pointing him out with an index finger but which, in a cowardly fashion, spared his life. No-one dared to stain their hands with that horrible blood. Some said, "He shouldn't have been born" and others said, "He ought to die," but no-one killed him. And nobody appreciated the good he did their brothers who, in sparing his life, felt understanding and generous. Everything remained the same. Everything would remain the same always: the woman beating against the boards. And in a precise instant at dawn, when he was crouching down in the darkness, he realised up to what point all the incantations, all the litanies and the rosaries were worthless: "He ought to die," repeated ad infinitum, would not provide a result. But for a moment he felt with him the reconciliation of suicide. And the world was wiped from his eyes. And he did not have to smile before the Ateneo Bookshop.

Buenos Aires
15-16 July, 1973

TEXAS, 1982

I know that Nancy will be seated in the living room now, in her house in Virginia, watching those beings that appear before her and who will follow her on her journey with Ben, from Norfolk to the West, on Highway 58, passing through Emporia and South Hill, flowing into Highway 85 South, passing through Durham, in North Carolina, crossing the western tip of South Carolina, entering Georgia through Lawrenceville to continue on to Atlanta; bumping into Montgomery at Alabama and taking Highway 65 South up to Mobile; taking Highway 10 West that becomes Highway 12 between Pearl River and Baton Rouge, and in New Orleans itself, carry on along 10 up to San Antonio and once in Texas, to follow Highway 35 South up to Dilley, the end of the itinerary, the smallest point on the large expansion; I approach the living room where Nancy is seated, immobile, on the mahogany rocking chair, waiting to watch the parade; her tiny body is now silence and stillness; this is my chance, the chance to reduce my skin until it is the same size as hers and to enter her and to place my eyes at the same height as hers and to watch too, hidden in her shape, that world that up till now was closed to me

I

they begin to arrive, they suddenly appear, right in the middle of the living room, taking possession of it as if it were the scenery in a theatre: some stroll about, others are sitting down; they are people from our time, wearing clothing from our time, but with a strange air about them, as if they belonged to another dimension; they could be Americans, perhaps from Ohio or from Missouri; with slow, immutable diligence, they wander, they have always wandered; an enormous family, fourteen in total; a young boy with blue eyes, in overalls, as if he had been displaced from a Mark Twain story to remain forever in this living room with the constant indication of being ready to go fishing; two more boys, with their outlines almost dim; three adolescent girls sharing between them a world which I cannot reach; two younger girls, with their soft curly hair, occupied in the act of dressing a doll; a baby in diapers seated on the ground, with his arms extended, as if he wanted to hug a shape in the atmosphere that is invisible to me; two young men who are entering their twenties, seated at a table, each holding a spoon, motionless in the air, ready to dig into the plate of lentils; an old woman seated on a taburete, a wooden chair with the cowhide back and seat, wearing her apron, a daisy hat covering her grey hair, gathered in a braid; a man, petrified in his maturity, in the grey that advances through his temple, petrified in his role as father of the family; and walking, strolling, tirelessly, a fifty year old woman, with her bun tucked into the nape of her neck, her reddish, chestnut hair interwoven with grey, and those long steps, slow, so eternal, and those eyes fixed on nothing that at that moment seem to look towards me, and I can almost shudder from my hiding place within the other skin, and my hands almost move forward when I attempt to gesture within the rigidity of those other hands anchored to the hard wood of the rocking chair

II

entering South Hill, Virginia, Highway 85 South, and suddenly, without the road vanishing, a persistent corner appears, with a building that could be an old pharmacy, a combination of pharmacy and soda fountain and three little girls holding hands and dancing around the lamp post; the eldest, about twelve years old, is nearly blonde, they are all nearly blonde; in one of their turns they let go of their hands, they line up on the sidewalk and start to jump to the rhythm of an invisible jump rope; the eldest, with a quick movement, swings her many skirts and allows a glimpse, for an instant, of her bloomers, made of white cotton, finished off with lace down to her knees

III

arriving at Spartanburg, on the Western tip of South Carolina, a huge, rectangular canvas appears, suspended in midair, with a Roman soldier standing out from it, as if disinterred from the waist up, twisting in pain, twisting slowly, trying to free himself from the impossibility of the grey canvas that keeps him suspended against the grey sky that matches the opaque grey of his helmet, his grey lance, the grey of his shield with which he beats his knees, the grey piece of his uniform that covers his chest

IV

South Carolina, near Greenville; an enormous wall of white marble appears on which the ivy climbs; perpendicular to the wall, a white marble floor, I don't see any tombstones, there must be tombstones in this scene, but I only see this woman that appears dressed in a dark grey skirt, a clear grey blouse, so thin, so desolate, reaching out towards me with her arms, begging mercy with this gesture, a little pity for her sadness

V

still on Route 85, a few kilometres from Lawrenceville, in Georgia, a woman appears before the car which continues to devour speed, stretches of road; from the seat, through the glass, I make out the woman's right hand on the front part of the hood, detaining the car, her left hand raised in the air, warning with a gesture that she reiterates vocally: no, Nancy, don't go on, stop, you must stop here, you must break the danger

VI

Ben remains comfortably settled, concentrating on his driving, aloof and detached from the story Nancy attempted to share with him, these visions that follow her from Norfolk until now, nearly arriving at Lawrenceville; from my hiding place, I receive the thought from her mind superimposed on mine: proof, I just want some proof, I want to tear the thick planetary smoke, to see what is beyond the distance where faces begin to appear, shapes that could just as well be visual games, simple cloud formations; she allowed her gaze to return to the level of the car's hood, to the level of the road and she remembered the woman's hand and voice: you must stop here, you must break the danger; without paying much attention to her own suggestion, Nancy points out a sign that announces the proximity of a motel, "perhaps it would be better to spend the night here;" within seconds, in the close night, a bolt of lightening hits the earth near the car; I feel the sudden stop, I leave her skin to penetrate the humidity of the rain, I follow them for a few moments, I hear the voice of the receptionist: "you were lucky you stopped here, a few kilometres more and you would have died in the floods, everything is flooded, there are kilometres of flooded roads;" I saw them move away down the corridors of the motel, Ben, gently knocking the

key between his fingers; Nancy, thinking that this was all
a coincidence, that there was no reason to think that her
impulse to halt their journey was brought about by an act
of salvation; I moved off carrying in my eyes the vision of
other dimensions that filtered through her eyes, into mine;
and I imagined them taking that route again, on the crystal
clear day on which Dilley would wait for them there, in the
West, filled with sun